First

a crescent chronicles novella

ALYSSA ROSE IVY

Cover Design: Once Upon a Time Covers

Editing: Final-Edits

Formatted by IRONHORSE Formatting

ISBN: 1495433161
ISBN-13: 978-1495433160

OTHER BOOKS BY ALYSSA ROSE IVY

Flight (The Crescent Chronicles #1)
Focus (The Crescent Chronicles #2)
Found (The Crescent Chronicles #3)
The Hazards of Skinny Dipping (Hazards)
Shaken Not Stirred (Mixology)
Derailed (Clayton Falls)
Veer (Clayton Falls)
Wrecked (Clayton Falls)
Beckoning Light (The Afterglow Trilogy #1)
Perilous Light (The Afterglow Trilogy #2)
Enduring Light (The Afterglow Trilogy #3)
Soar (The Empire Chronicles #1)

To my readers:
Thanks for taking this journey with me.

CHAPTER ONE

"Looks like tonight's activity just arrived." Jared's comment made me snap my head up from the bar. The only activities my friend cared about involved girls—he had my attention.

It didn't take long to see what caught his eye. She was gorgeous—especially those long tan legs that were shown off nicely in the short yellow dress she wore. Slim but clearly athletic, I could only imagine how much fun she'd be.

I finished off my Jack and Coke, slamming the empty glass down on the mahogany bar. The new guy who'd bought the place had gone to town on the hunk of wood. I doubted he had any idea that the hotel he'd purchased housed a hell of a lot more than rooms, food, and booze.

The girl walked around the lobby like she owned the place, her eyes taking in every detail. Finally they found me, and I got a look at her bright green eyes. I gave her my trademark smile. It worked every time. She smiled back, and I nodded, telling her to come over. I thought she was going to, until she shook her head and kept on walking. She didn't even give me a second glance. What the hell?

So focused on her retreating figure, I was barely aware of Jared talking. "I call dibs on the blonde."

"Blonde? She was a brunette." He must have been losing it.

My other friend, Owen, laughed. "There were two girls, Levi."

"Oh, I only noticed the one." Had there really been someone else with her?

Jared smirked. "You seriously didn't notice that blonde? That top didn't leave much to the imagination."

"Did you see where they went?" I really didn't care about the blonde, but I had to find Miss Legs. I couldn't believe she'd blown me off like that. Maybe I was right—she was going to be a lot of fun.

"They're probably in the courtyard." Owen yawned. He seriously worried me sometimes. A girl dumped him, and he'd practically been a monk since. The guy needed to get laid. Jared and I were going to have to try harder to get him out there.

"I could really use a night with that one." I turned to Owen. Our taste in women had always been more similar. Jared only went for busty blondes, where as I wanted the brunettes with the long legs. A nice chest didn't hurt—not at all, but a short skirt on the right girl could drive me crazy.

"I noticed her." Owen's small smile would have been enough for me to let him have her usually, but this one was for me.

"I've got to find her. She might even be worth a second night." Or a third.

Owen snorted. "Real nice."

I shrugged. "Just saying."

Jared finished his drink. "We'll find them, but we need to get moving. Your dad's going to get pissed if we're late."

"Yeah, I know." I left a twenty on the bar and took one last glance around to make sure she hadn't changed her mind and come back, before I walked over to the elevator. I smirked at the weird bellboy that was always staring at us. He took a step back and lowered his eyes.

Once the doors shut, I inserted the key card and pushed the button for the basement. The central offices and chambers of the Society were housed on a level of the hotel that wasn't supposed to exist. It was better for everyone if humans didn't go looking for us. When you're a prince of a supernatural society, you understand the importance of keeping some things secret.

"What do you think he wants us for this time?" Jared asked, leaning back against the wall.

"Like I'd know, but he didn't sound happy." I listened to one message, but it was only the latest of many. My dad's calls were always the same. Either I'd done something wrong, or I was about to do something wrong.

Jared stuffed his hands in the pockets of his jeans. "I guess we'll find out."

The elevator doors opened, depositing us into a room that would be dark for the average person, but we had no problem seeing. One of the benefits of being a Pteron was perfect night vision. I pushed open the doors, and we headed toward my dad's office, which was located just off the main chamber.

I knocked on the door loudly. "Who is it?" Dad called.

I knocked one last time just to be a pain. "Who do you think?"

"Come in, Levi." His low, gravelly voice always sounded pissed when he talked to me.

I walked in, Owen and Jared followed behind.

Dad didn't glance up from the paperwork on his desk. "Close the door."

Jared slammed the door harder than he needed to. The action wasn't lost on my dad. He finally dropped the paperwork, and his glare had Jared standing up straighter.

Dad didn't miss a beat. His steely gaze moved to me. "You missed last night's council meeting."

"What are you talking about? We just met last week."

"I called an emergency meeting last night." He ran a hand through his gray hair. At one time, it had been the same shade of brown as mine, but time, or too many years as the King of The Society had aged him.

Shit. I should have listened to the other messages. "Yeah, well, I didn't know."

"Is that all you have to say for yourself? Twenty-two years old, and you behave like a child."

My dad never minced words, but he usually kept his cool. Things had to be serious for him to be flipping out on me in front of my friends.

"I'm sorry. It won't happen again."

"It better not." His icy stare left little doubt he was serious.

"What did you discuss?" I shifted uneasily from foot to foot. Only my father had the ability to make me nervous. Most people were afraid of me or kissed up to me to get what they wanted. There were only four exceptions. Owen, Jared, and my parents.

"The Blackwells. There's talk of a takeover attempt."

"Like those Yankees could do anything," Jared spat. He never kept his mouth shut, not even in front of my father.

"Has your father taught you nothing, Jared? The second you start underestimating your opponent, you've lost your advantage."

"Yes, sir." Mentioning Jared's father usually had that effect. His dad was essentially the head of security for my family. We'd spent many nights getting wasted and talking about how much we hated our fathers. Neither of us would ever live up to their expectations.

"So what's the plan?" I slunk down in a high back chair. This could take a while.

"The plan is that you grow up and find a girl."

"This again? I'm not ready. Just because you and Mom got married at twenty doesn't mean I have to do it." I looked for a mate once and all it brought me was heartache. What was the point of torturing myself again? I'd put it off as long as I could.

"You're not twenty. You graduate college in less than a year; it's time to stop chasing after everything in a skirt. Find someone worth your time."

"What does this have to do with the takeover attempt?"

"Don't play stupid." His cold blue eyes locked on mine.

"No one cares whether I have a mate. They know I can have a kid, it's not a big deal."

"Everyone cares. Everyone." He cracked his knuckles. He only did that when he was particularly worried.

"I'll take a mate when I meet the right girl." I leaned back in my chair and stretched out my legs. Getting angry wasn't going to help the situation, but I was tired of this bullshit.

"You can't find her unless you look."

"He does plenty of looking," Owen mumbled under his breath.

"Looking for a mate is different from looking for a girl to jump in bed with. I'd have thought you'd understand that, Owen." Dad really liked to get you where it hurt.

"You told me I have until graduation. That's months from now." I planned to enjoy every last day of my freedom until then, starting with tonight. I needed to get out of the meeting so I could find the girl.

"Building a relationship takes time. Do you expect to meet someone and bind yourself to her the next day? Don't wait too long."

Jared sniggered. He went through women faster than I did.

"I'm tasking you two with making sure it happens. We all have a lot to lose if Levi can't keep his pants on long enough to find a worthy girl."

"Absolutely, sir." Of course Owen agreed immediately. He'd been kissing my father's ass for years.

"Can we please talk about the real plan? The one that doesn't involve my sex life."

Dad leaned his elbows on his desk. He looked tired. "All we can do is stay alert and make sure our own ranks are loyal. If things come to blow, we can't have any mutiny from within."

"I'm guessing my dad's already on that?" Jared asked.

"Yes. But I expect you all to do your part."

"Will do, sir." Even Jared knew that pushing my dad could have dire consequences.

"Good. Now get out of here. I have better things to do today." He went back to the paperwork. I wondered if it was anything real, or just an excuse to look busy.

"Bye, Dad. Great talking to you." I got the hell out of his office and back to the elevator. I was angry, and I could feel the transformation wanting to happen. I relaxed and pushed it back. I had other things to think about, namely Miss Legs.

CHAPTER TWO

I leaned back against the black leather couch in our house. I'd had the couch for two years, the same amount of time I'd lived in the place. As soon as freshman year ended, Jared, Owen, and I moved in there. One year in the dorms was more than enough for us.

With some distance, I was finally relaxing after the meeting with my dad. The man knew how to boil my blood, and it usually took time and copious amounts of alcohol to get back to normal. Nothing I did was ever good enough for him, and after twenty-two years, I was beyond tired of it.

"So where do you think those girls are?" I knew I was being ridiculous. There were plenty of attractive girls around, but there was something about her that got under my skin. I'd practically memorized every curve of her body in the seconds she'd been in view. She wouldn't be escaping from me so easily again.

Jared tossed me another beer from the fridge. "It's their first night in the French Quarter. They'll be at the Cat's Meow. They always go to the Cat's Meow."

"No way. She's not the type." I tried to picture her at a place like that. No, she was classier. She'd probably be looking for a lounge or something.

"Not the type?" Jared twisted off the top of his beer. "I guarantee they'll be there. I bet you fifty they'll sing karaoke."

Owen walked in, dumping three po' boys on the table. "Who? Those girls from the hotel? Yeah, I'm in on this. My bet is *Girl's Just Want to Have Fun*. They always sing that."

"No, I bet they're more the *Like a Virgin* types," Jared threw in.

"I'm game. But let's make it a hundred. I haven't washed either of you out in a while." Things were always more fun when there was money involved.

They both laughed. "All right, a hundred."

I dug into my shrimp po' boy, already planning out the evening. I'd find the girl and forget all about the bullshit with my dad.

The door burst open again, and the flash of red hair made it immediately clear who'd arrived.

"Have you ever heard of knocking?" Owen snapped at his little sister, Hailey.

"If you have a problem with it, lock the door." She swiped a Coke from the fridge. She had no problem making herself at home.

"Is there a reason you're gracing us with your presence?" I'd known Hailey her whole life and she was like a little sister—the annoying, won't ever leave you alone type. She was only three years younger than us, but sometimes it seemed like ten.

Hailey leaned back against the counter. "Yeah. I need Owen to talk to Dad."

"I doubt I'm going to, but about what?" Owen answered after finishing off his sandwich.

"He's making me request J.L. as a dorm. There is no way I'm living in an all-girls dorm!"

We all laughed. I still couldn't believe she was starting at Tulane in the fall. How was she old enough for college? I still pictured her playing with dolls even though one glance at her figure told you those days were long gone.

"Come on. This is so not fair." Hailey pouted. When she made faces like that, she only looked younger. I decided not to point it out to her. Giving her a hard time was fun, but you had to be careful not to push it too far. It wasn't worth her wrath.

"You can't be surprised." Owen tried to keep a straight face.

Hailey walked into the living room and took a seat on the arm of a couch. "So he caught me making out with a guy? It's not like I was sleeping with him."

Owen cringed, probably mentally picturing his sister hooking up with someone. "Hailey, Dad's always been protective. Inviting a guy over when they weren't home wasn't the smartest decision, but how could you be stupid enough to get caught? You always wait until you know they won't possibly come back." Owen said it snidely, but I think he actually felt bad. Their parents definitely treated them differently.

"So you really won't talk to him?" she whined.

Owen crumpled up the wrapper of his po' boy. "Living in a girl's dorm isn't that bad. It's nicer than a lot of the others."

"I guess." She slid down from the arm to a couch cushion. "I hope I at least get a cool roommate."

"Me too, because then maybe you won't show up here uninvited all the time." I couldn't resist. She was so easy to annoy.

"And don't worry, Hailey. I'd be more than happy to visit your new friends anytime." Jared winked.

9

"Arrgh! You guys are useless. Thanks for nothing." She stormed out just the way she arrived.

Owen got up, pushing back his chair. "Seriously, how am I related to her?"

Jared collected our plates and brought them to the sink. No one would believe how much of a neat freak he was. "I don't know, she's hot and you're ugly as shit." He grinned.

"Don't even start."

I laughed. My roommates were definitely entertaining.

CHAPTER THREE

"You better be ready to pay up," Owen taunted. We'd spent the better part of an hour searching the Quarter. After striking out at the classier lounges and bars, I didn't want to admit that my friends were probably right. I finally gave in, and we walked into the Cat's Meow. It had been a while since I'd dragged myself into that place. It's not like it was much worse than the rest of the Bourbon Street bars, but you also had to suffer through horrible singing. The current song was no exception.

I looked over toward the stage and, sure enough, there they were, singing *Girls Just Want to Have Fun*. I had really misread her, or maybe it was the friend who convinced her to come. "Fine, I'll get you your money later."

It's not like I cared about two hundred bucks. The important part was that I'd found the girl. Mmm, yes, and she was wearing a short skirt. So maybe singing wasn't her strong suit, but she looked good doing it.

I bought a beer and went ahead and got a shot for her. I had a feeling she was going to need it when she was done. There was something about her expression that said she wasn't having as much fun as she was pretending to. But I was. Hell, I was having a great time. That jean skirt was so short. I got a real nice view.

"Are you sure they're legal?" Leave it to Owen to ask such a dumb question.

"Yeah, they've got to be eighteen."

He frowned. "You sure? Do you really want to mess with jail bait?"

"Shit, Owen, they're not kids. They got in here, didn't they?" Jared argued.

I tried to ignore them. I was still enjoying my view.

"They could have fakes. But it's your problem, not mine."

"Exactly, go find your own. Or wait, you don't do girls anymore." Jared smirked.

"Shut the fuck up."

"Both of you shut up." The song ended, and I watched as the girls jumped off the stage. I waited until they separated to make my move.

She was definitely flustered, not even paying attention to where she was going. I walked directly into her path.

"You look like you could use this." I pushed the shot into her hand.

She looked up at me, and I saw the recognition in her eyes. She remembered me. She nodded and then downed the shot.

"What was that?" She coughed a little. I probably could have gotten her something tamer, but what would have been the fun in that?

"A jaeger shot." I laughed. "Feeling better?"

"Yeah. I can't believe I did that." She looked back over her shoulder, like she was making sure the stage was still there.

"It really wasn't so bad. It was more entertaining than if Cyndi Lauper performed it herself." Much more entertaining. I looked at her up close for the first time. I watched as a few drops of sweat ran down from her neck and disappeared into her tank top. She had a nicer chest than I originally thought. Add in her killer legs and she was hotter than any girl I'd ever seen.

"So, thanks for the shot, but I need to find my friend."

"Hey, you can't run off on me again." If she thought she was getting away this time, she had another thing coming. She was mine. "Besides, your friend appears to be unavailable."

Surprisingly, Jared didn't already have her in a corner somewhere. She was occupied by some guy who looked like he was in town for a conference. I knew the type. He was looking to score, have a story to run home with. The blonde was drunk enough he might just get lucky.

"Run off on you again? That implies we've run into each other before."

So she was going to play that game?

"I saw you at the Crescent City Hotel this afternoon, but you took off before I could say hello." I leaned in closer, using the blaring music as an excuse, even though I could hear perfectly well. Damn, she even smelled good. I didn't recognize the perfume—but it was light, the right kind.

"Oh, I didn't notice you."

It was time to act interested in her life. "You here for vacation?"

"I'm here for work, actually, at the hotel." She flipped some of her long brown hair off her shoulder.

"Are you around for the whole summer then?" Not the tourist I expected. If the sex was as good as I knew it would be, a longer stay could be convenient.

"Yeah, I'm here until I start school in the fall." So Owen wasn't completely off. She was probably fresh out of high school.

"All right, so where are you going to school?"

"Princeton." She tried to hide a smile. She was proud, but didn't want me to know it.

"Nice." Smart girls weren't necessarily bad, as long as they didn't overanalyze everything.

"You in school?"

"Yeah, I'm going to be a senior at Tulane." Maybe she'd loosen up a little if she realized I was in school. Some girls were like that. They assumed you were a good guy if you were in college. It made no sense, but it usually worked.

"Oh, so you live here?"

"Born and raised."

"I didn't think locals hung out at places like this."

"We don't usually, but they're great spots to meet girls from out of town." Or more specifically, it was a good spot to find her.

She shook her head. "Ah, so you're one of them."

"One of who?" I tried to figure out what group she was throwing me in with.

"The type to prey on innocent tourists."

"Innocent tourists? You make me sound like the big bad wolf."

"And you're not?" She got a twinkle in her eye.

A wolf? As if she was dealing with something that tame. "Only if you're Red Riding Hood." I'd pretend to be a wolf if it involved her.

"Wow, that's original," she said sarcastically, but her face gave her away. She was definitely interested. "Well, nice talking to you."

What? Was she seriously trying to blow me off again? I had to act fast. "Hey, I didn't even get your name yet."

"Allie."

"Is that short for Allison?" I needed to keep her talking.

"Yes, but no one calls me Allison."

"I'm Levi." I held out my hand.

"Is that short for something?" She gave me her hand and it felt nice in mine. I didn't want to end the contact. I liked touching her, but I finally dropped it.

"Leviathan. But you can call me whatever you like." Hell, she could call me a wolf if she was doing it in my bed.

"Well, nice to meet you." She actually started to walk away. What the hell was going on?

"Wow, it's hotel bar guy." The blonde swayed as she walked over drunkenly. Either she was a light weight or she'd had more to drink than Allie. Allie—it was nice to have a name to go with those long legs.

"So you did notice me." I leaned in closer to Allie again. If she'd noticed me enough to talk to her friend, I was good to go. She was just playing hard to get. I didn't mind a good game of chase.

"So, does that mean you changed your mind?" the blonde asked.

"Changed her mind? About what?" Had she talked about me more?

"Allie's sworn off men, or so she claims." Blondie took a swig from her beer. If she drank much more, she'd pass out before anyone got her home.

"Is that so?" What did that mean exactly? I'd have thought she was into girls, but I wasn't getting that vibe.

Allie exhaled loudly. "Yes, not that it's any of your business."

"Any particular reason why?" I was intrigued. Had someone hurt her? I felt an unfamiliar feeling of protectiveness take hold. I shook it off.

"None that I wish to explain."

"She thinks it's because she has bad luck with relationships, but really it's because no one is good enough for her," Blondie tattled. Allie's eyes got all big—I got myself ready for a cat fight.

But then Allie relaxed her shoulders. "I think I need another drink."

"My pleasure. What can I get you?"

"Surprise me." There was nothing overly flirtatious in her voice, but I still took her willingness to trust me with the task as a good sign.

"I will." I winked at her. "I'm good at surprises."

I needed to find the perfect drink. Allie seemed like the kind of girl who liked them strong and sweet. I ordered her something different, my own invention. I called it the Oasis. I heard the girls continuing to argue. One of the many benefits of enhanced hearing was eavesdropping in on conversations. The blonde's name was Jess, and she was really egging Allie on.

As I returned to the girls, Jared caught my eye. He and Owen were sitting at a table across the room. He nodded, wanting us to come over. Normally, I'd have made him get off his ass, but I wanted Allie's attention, which meant getting her friend fixated on someone else.

"A few of my friends are sitting over there. Care to join us?"

Jess glanced over and answered first. "Why not?" Her words were casual but it was obvious she was interested in one of my friends. I hoped it was Owen— that would make tonight interesting.

Allie still hadn't said anything, so I looked to her. She finally nodded, and we walked over.

I made the introductions. "Girls, this is Jared and Owen. And this is Allie and Jess." I realized afterward that they might have thought it was odd that I knew Jess' name, but they didn't seem to notice.

"Well, hello there." Jared grinned. He looked over Allie, but then moved his attention to Jess.

Owen just nodded. "Hey." He smiled again, but I didn't worry about it. He knew not to get in the way of what I wanted.

Jess sat down next to Jared. He must have been the one who caught her eye. I'd hoped she'd keep Owen occupied so he'd stop looking at Allie, but it didn't actually matter.

I put down our drinks and pulled out a chair for Allie, careful to make sure she sat in the one closest to the wall. I wanted her attention all to myself. "You can't really mean to punish the entire male gender for the errors of a few."

I watched her pick up her drink and taste it. Her whole body responded to the sip. Her shoulders relaxed and she leaned back against her chair. She liked it, and I liked her smile. It went all the way to her eyes.

"Because it would be really unfair to do that."

"Um, can we please talk about something else?" She turned away from me, and I saw her looking at Owen. Not what I was hoping for.

"Sure, for now. What made you decide to take the job at the hotel?"

Her shoulders tensed up a little again. "Oh, I needed a job and my dad was able to get it for me."

Jess leaned over the table toward me. "Because Allie's dad is super rich and bought the place." Whoa. This was the new owner's daughter? I wasn't sure what to make of the information. "What? It's true."

I must have missed an exchange between the girls. Was Allie trying to keep it a secret? Most girls would brag about something like that.

"Your dad bought the Crescent City Hotel?" Jared sat up straighter. He seriously needed to keep his cool.

"Yeah. The deal went through earlier this year." Allie downed her drink. Something about this conversation was stressing her out. I wanted to find out what it was. I doubted she knew anything about the hotel. It was something else.

I wasn't about to ask her about it. I'd just have to find out another way. She set down her empty glass.

"I guess you liked it?"

"Maybe a little. What was it?" She ran her finger over the edge of the glass.

"Want another?"

"No, don't worry about it. I can get one for myself if you'll tell me what it is." I could practically see the wheels turning in her head. She was the type of girl who worried about guys buying her drinks. She was afraid that meant she owed them something. Such bullshit. Buying a drink for a girl was just an opening. Where it went after that depended on her.

"I'm getting up anyway. Besides, if you don't know what it is, you'll have to let me keep buying them for you." I enjoyed the look of annoyance that flashed across her face. I pushed back my chair without giving her a chance to argue.

"Don't worry. She's not always so uptight." Jess' voice surprised me as I ordered some more drinks. I hadn't expected Jared and Jess to follow me. That left Allie alone with Owen—not the plan—definitely not the plan.

"I'm not worried about it," I said offhandedly, wanting the bartender to move faster. This was taking far too long. Owen was laughing. What could she be saying? At least she didn't look as amused.

"Levi's good at, uh, breaking through tough exteriors." Jared ordered them a couple of shots.

"She's worth it," Jess said as I walked away. I couldn't read Jess. One moment she was egging her friend on and the next she was talking her up. I ignored the comment and kept walking. I'd been away from the table long enough.

"It looked like you two were having a good conversation. Did I miss anything?" I shot Owen an annoyed look. He was seriously beginning to piss me off.

Allie glanced up at me. "Nothing worth repeating."

Owen smiled. "Well, Allie was telling me that she isn't interested in you."

Hmm, well at least they were talking about me.

I took my seat and leaned in close to her, letting her know what I thought of the statement. "It's because she's sworn off men. But I think I'll just have to be the exception."

She took a few sips of the new drink. "What in the world would make you think that you would be an exception?"

"One, you're attracted to me, and two, I can be very persistent."

She tightened her grip on the glass. "I am not attracted to you!"

"Like hell you're not," Jess said before bursting into laughter. She hadn't even sat down yet.

"You know there could be a few females alive that aren't into you, Levi," Jared mocked. I was ready to knock that smirk off his face.

"It's always a possibility, but that's not the case this time. She likes me, she just won't admit it." I scooted my chair closer to her.

She sighed and closed her eyes. She seemed pretty stressed out, and I wanted to do something about that. I put an arm around her shoulder. It felt nice, natural.

I moved close enough that I could kiss her, but I resisted. It wasn't time yet. She moved to turn away but I caught her chin, making her look up at me. "Stop looking away. I love green eyes."

"Does that line usually work for you?"

"Usually. I'm guessing it's not going to work tonight."

Her lips quirked into just a hint of a smile. "Not a chance."

"I'll just have to get more creative." As frustrating as her resistance was, it was also a nice change of pace. It would make finally getting her in bed all the more worth it.

"You do that." Her look was teasing. She was definitely challenging me.

"So, what do you think of New Orleans so far?" Owen asked her, having to pull her attention away again.

Jess answered. "It's been fantastic. It's so awesome to get away and meet new people."

"And what about you, Allie?" I asked, finding I actually cared about her answer.

"Well, considering we've been here less than twenty-four hours, it's hard to have much of an impression, but I like it so far."

I leaned in again. "You'll have to keep me posted as you have more time to form an opinion."

"I'll be sure to keep you updated."

I thought there might be a promise in her words, but that might have just been wishful thinking. The game of chase was fun, but I was ready to move things forward.

"You girls want to see the rest of the Quarter?" Jared was just looking for an excuse to get Jess to leave with him. The conference guy from earlier was watching her. She didn't seem to notice. Jared definitely had her attention.

"Yes!" Jess squeaked. "We haven't seen anything but here and the hotel."

"You interested?" I whispered in Allie's ear. I liked how it made her shiver a little. I definitely had an effect on her.

"Sure. Why not?" She finished off her drink and stood up. She tugged down on her skirt. I had to resist the urge to reach out and stop her. The skirt was fine the way it was.

I put an arm around her, leading her out. I shot Owen a backward glance to let him know to stay away. "I guarantee you're going to love New Orleans."

She slipped away from me. I held in a frustrated sigh.

"Is that right?" She sounded distracted, and I noticed her staring at her friend and Jared. Was she worried about her?

We walked down St. Peter Street and crossed over into Jackson Square. Allie seemed entranced by it. I noticed her eyeing the wrought iron railings. That was the second time I'd noticed her admiring architecture. Maybe we had that interest in common.

We maneuvered through the square, past the usual crowd of musicians and artists showing off their work.

"Care to have your fortune read?" a palm reader called out.

"No, thanks." Allie waved her off.

I let my arm brush against hers. "Are you sure you don't want a glimpse into your future?"

"I prefer surprises." Her response seemed at odds with how uptight she'd been most of the night. I sensed there was a lot more to her I still wasn't seeing.

"Same here," Jess agreed. "This is too cool. It might be even better than Washington Square Park."

Washington Square? So they were New Yorkers.

"Of course, this is just where all the tourists hang out. There are much cooler places, hon. Maybe I'll show you sometime," Jared crooned.

"Like where, your apartment?" Allie raised an eyebrow. She had a nice sense of humor.

"Why, you want to see my place?" he threw back at her.

"In your dreams."

I laughed. She had some nerve. I couldn't resist touching her. I came up from behind her and wrapped my arms around her waist. She fit perfectly. "Would you change your mind about that if you knew I was his roommate?"

"Why would that change my mind?" She pushed away. I reluctantly released her.

Maybe I needed to give her space so she'd come to me. Her game was wearing on me, but it was only going to end one way. With her in my bed.

I tried to pay attention to everything else going on, but then, of course, Owen had to go talk to her again. Pushing my annoyance aside, I listened in. They were talking about a crow on the fence. She seemed to find the bird creepy, and I wondered what she'd think if she knew what I was. When I heard them talking about going home, I had to intervene. She was thanking Owen for giving her a heads up.

"The heads up on what?"

"I was simply suggesting she pry Jess away from Jared if she wants to get her home tonight."

"What's the hurry? The night is young." I smiled at her, resisting the urge to punch Owen. If I wasn't good at controlling myself, my eyes would have changed.

"We have our first day of work tomorrow."

"Your first day of work at your father's hotel. Can't you skip out?" I was definitely not ready to say goodnight, and it was looking unlikely she was coming home with me.

"No! I am not missing my first day of work. I'm not like that."

If I couldn't have her that night, I'd just have to try again. "Really? Maybe I can learn more about you tomorrow night? Maybe over dinner?"

"Not a chance."

"Oh, that's right; you think you've sworn off men."

She pretended to ignore me, but I saw the tiny curl of her lips. "Jess, let's go!"

"Now? Seriously?" Jess whined.

"I'm sure you can meet up with your friend another time."

Her friend? Allie had a bit of edge, didn't she?

"What's the rush all of a sudden?" Jared asked, glaring at Allie.

"Owen decided to point out the late hour to her." I knew Jared would appreciate it as much as I did.

"What the hell, man?" Jared lunged at Owen, his eyes turning black. I hoped the girls didn't notice, and I put myself between my friends. We'd have to settle this later.

"Let it go, Jared. I'm sure we'll have plenty of opportunities to see them again. We'll walk you girls home." I wasn't happy to see Allie leave, but I also wanted another chance. It was time to cut our losses and regroup.

When we reached the hotel, Allie waved. "Goodnight."

"I'll be seeing you," I said before walking away. I'm sure she had no clue how true my words were—there wasn't a chance in the world I was letting this girl go.

CHAPTER FOUR

Miraculously, Jared didn't kill Owen. Jared was usually reasonable, but if you cock blocked him, you needed to be ready for his wrath. They'd stopped fighting long enough to go to sleep, but that didn't mean Jared wasn't still angry the next day. I poured myself a cup of coffee and watched as they stared each other down in the kitchen.

"Are you guys going to survive if I leave for a few hours?" I wasn't in a rush to go anywhere, but I didn't have a choice.

"If you're going to stalk that girl from last night, I'm going to have to intervene." Jared laughed.

"I'm not stalking anyone." Even if I did want to see her again. "My grandparents are in town. I've been ordered to attend a family lunch at my parents' house."

"Oh. Lucky you." Jared popped open the top on a can of Coke. "I'd offer to join you, but I'd rather go to the dentist."

"Your family isn't that bad." Owen seemed relieved Jared had moved on from threatening his life. "If you need company, I'll suffer along with you."

"I appreciate the sacrifice, but that's not going to fly with Georgina." My grandmother was pretty intense, and a family lunch was limited to family. No exceptions.

"Call us when you get out."

"If I get out," I mumbled as I walked to the door. "Try not to kill each other while I'm gone."

Jared laughed. "I'm over it. We'll go out later and find someone else."

"Yeah, maybe." I left before he could question me. I was already late to see my family. I didn't feel like explaining to my friends that I didn't want to find another girl. Until I got Allie into bed, no one else was going to cut it.

I parked my black BMW along the curb in front of my parents' large white house. With a wraparound porch and tall columns, it fit the southern style you would expect to see in the Garden District. After sitting in the car longer than necessary, I got out and headed to the front door. There was no reason to further delay the inevitable, and hopefully the afternoon would go by quickly.

My mom opened the door before I could ring the bell. I still had a key, but I never used it anymore. "Hey, honey." The stress on her face could only mean one thing. Georgina had already arrived.

"Hi, Mom. Sorry I'm late."

"It's fine."

"It's fine?" My grandmother strode into the entryway. Tall and always impeccably dressed, my grandmother was nothing like most women her age. She was so full of energy and ready to jump on any mistake, she could intimidate any woman or man. My grandfather was included in that. I guess some might find it comical that the former King of the Society was terrified of his very human wife.

"Hi, Grandma. Sorry about that."

"It's all right, Leviathan. You learned your manners from your mother. I can't blame you." She gave me a light hug while glaring at my mom.

"It's not Mom's fault."

"Sure. Maybe not this time."

Mom gave me a "don't make it worse" look. I nodded. She was right. Nothing I could say was going to make it better. Besides, she'd start in on me soon enough.

"Where's Dad?" I assumed he was in his study, but I figured it was worth asking. Escaping from Georgina's eye for a few minutes was usually worth facing my father alone.

"He's working. Let's talk." Georgina took my arm and led me toward the living room. My mother didn't follow. I didn't blame her.

I took a seat in a beige arm chair. Georgina sat down caddy corner on a matching couch.

"How was your trip?" I decided to start with the niceties. That would give her less time to grill me about my life.

"Don't bother, Leviathan. We both know why I'm here."

I grinned. "To spend time with your adoring family?"

"I take it you haven't made any more progress with finding a mate?" She leaned forward slightly.

I exhaled loudly. "What's the rush?"

"What's the rush? As though you don't know the consequences if you fail to have an heir."

I pictured what I'd get to do with Allie to make an heir. I quickly pushed that thought away. I was only a few feet from my grandmother. "I'll have a kid eventually."

"You've met someone." Her lips curved into a small smile. "Out with it."

"What?" I sat up with a start. Had I said something out loud?

She cast me a warning glance. "Don't lie to me. You were day dreaming about someone."

"I don't day dream."

"I expect to meet her soon." She folded her hands in her lap.

"There's no one to meet." I didn't even have a real date lined up with Allie, and I was thinking about getting her into bed, not binding her to me as my lifelong mate.

"If there's no one, would you like me to introduce you to a few candidates? I know of several young women who might be worthy of your hand."

"No!" I shot up out of my chair. There was no way my grandmother was playing matchmaker. "I'll pick my own mate."

"Then do it." She stood and hugged me again. As she turned to leave the room, she whispered, "You'll know it if you find her." Her voice was low, but she wanted me to hear. I didn't need to listen to any of that again.

I suffered through lunch. My grandmother only criticized my mother's cooking once, but the conversation was awkward and no one wanted to be there. My father barely said two words to me. I knew he was still pissed about me missing the meeting. As soon as I finished, I excused myself from the table and went up to my childhood bedroom.

The room was sparsely furnished and decorated, exactly the way it had been when I was a kid. My father didn't believe that boys should bother with anything but the basics. Toys and posters would only get in the way. I walked past my king sized bed, still covered in the blue comforter I'd grown up with, before stopping in front of my dresser. I pulled open my sock drawer and searched around until I found the small ring. I'd freaked out when my father gave me the ring that was intended for my mate. Seven years later and the ruby-covered ring still scared me. I ran my fingers over the stones, stuffing it in my pocket when I heard a knock on the door.

I turned to face my mom in the doorway. "Hey, Mom." She was the one member of the family I actually got along with.

"You doing all right up here? You were really quiet at lunch." Her warm eyes studied my face. She was worried about me.

"Am I ever talkative at these things?"

She strode over to me. "No, but you're going to be king soon. You're going to have to get better at controlling your feelings."

"And I need to find a mate. Isn't that what the theme of the day is?"

"No. You don't need to find *a* mate." She gave me a long look.

"I don't?" That was news.

"You need to find *the right* mate." She patted me on the shoulder. "Think about that."

"Is it okay if I leave?"

"Sure. Just slip out the back."

"Thanks." I gave her a quick hug before taking the back stairs two at a time. It wasn't until I was in my car that I realized I hadn't put the ring back.

CHAPTER FIVE

I owed Jared. Short of stalking the hotel to look for her or talking to my contacts, I had no immediate way to see Allie again. Lucky for me, Jess had happily slipped her number to Jared. All it took was one phone call, and the plans were set. From what I gathered, Allie hadn't been part of the planning, but that didn't worry me. She could play hard to get all she wanted. At the end of the night, she'd be coming home with me.

We waited in front of the elevators. I'd never picked up a girl at the hotel before, but my assumption was they weren't taking the stairs down. After waiting a few minutes, the doors opened, and I remembered why I was putting in all the effort. Allie looked even hotter than last time. She wore a pink halter style dress that accentuated her green eyes. Like everything else I'd seen her in, it was short, and she kept it casual with flip flops. I liked that she wasn't the kind of girl who wore heels all the time. Heels could be hot, but a pair of flip flops meant a girl was laid back.

"Hey there, Allison." I purposely used her full name to see what kind of response I got.

"It's Allie." She feigned annoyance, but I noticed her studying my chest and arms.

I smiled, letting her know I'd caught her in the act of checking me out. "Oh yeah, I forgot."

"I'm sure." She shook her head, bringing my attention to her hair. I wanted to run my hands through those brown locks. I also wanted them sprawled out on my pillow.

"Are you girls ready to see uptown?" Owen addressed both of them. I got the sense he was being careful. Smart guy.

Allie adjusted her purse on her shoulder. "Sure, should we follow you or get an address for my GPS?"

"Neither." I put a hand on the small of her back and led her toward the door. "We're taking the streetcar. That way you don't have to worry about a designated driver."

"Will it still be running when we need to get home?" She seemed worried. Wasn't she from New York? Did New Orleans at night scare her that much? She didn't need to worry about anything with me around.

"This is New Orleans. It runs all night." Jared didn't bother to sugar coat his annoyance at her. He wasn't an Allie fan for some reason, but it wasn't my problem.

I stayed close to Allie's side as we walked the few blocks to the corner of Canal and St. Charles. We caught the streetcar just before it pulled away. Allie struggled to slip a dollar bill into the machine, and I pushed her hand away. She wasn't paying for anything when she was with me. "I've got this."

The car lurched forward and Allie lost her balance. I caught her easily in my arms. "Easy does it, darling." I inhaled her warm sweet scent. She wore the same perfume again. After detangling herself from my arms, she held onto the seats as she walked down the aisle.

She'd barely settled into a seat when I slid in right next to her.

"So where are we going exactly?" She looked over me to watch Jess and Jared. I may have had my work cut out for me, but Jared had a guarantee going for him.

I pulled her attention away from them. "The Maple Leaf. It's a bar that always has great live music. You're going to like it."

She rested a hand on her leg. "Glad to know you are now an expert on what I like."

"I'm an expert on a lot of things." I stretched out my legs, brushing my leg against hers in the process. Her body tensed ever so slightly, but it wasn't in a bad way.

She gazed out the window, and I was glad it was a clear night out. The windows on the streetcar were open, providing a nice breeze. I needed it with the way my body heated around her. She felt it too. I know she did. There was an electricity sizzling between us like nothing I'd ever experienced before. I wanted her so bad it hurt.

I followed her gaze. She was checking out the houses lining St. Charles. "Beautiful, aren't they?" I leaned in close and smiled when I noticed the goose bumps forming on her exposed shoulder. Considering the heat, I knew I was the cause of them.

She took a moment to answer. "The homes? Yeah, they're gorgeous. Is this the Garden district?"

"Yes. Home sweet home."

"Have you always lived here?" she asked absently, probably deciding which house she'd want for herself.

"Born and raised, and I never want to move anywhere else." I also had no choice. New Orleans would always be my home.

She turned away from the window and her face was mere inches from mine. "Really?"

I fought the urge to taste her lips. I couldn't rush the moment and lose my chance. "Does that really surprise you?"

"I mean, you told me you were from here, but don't most people our age want to explore new places?"

If she only knew how tied to New Orleans I was. At the moment, I couldn't have cared less where I was though. The company was all I needed. "Why explore when you have everything you need right here?"

"Yeah. Whatever." She turned away again, but I didn't miss her lingering glance. I let her enjoy the view until we reached our stop.

I touched her leg gently. "This is us." I pulled the cord to request a stop, then I led her off the car. "It's just a few blocks from here."

We'd only made it a few steps when Jess walked between us and grabbed Allie's hand. "Have a nice ride?"

"Splendid." Allie's face was slightly flushed.

Jess grinned. "It looked like you were enjoying yourself."

I laughed. Obviously, I wasn't the only one who picked up on it.

Allie gave it right back to her. "Yeah, I wouldn't have thought you noticed. You looked pretty distracted yourself."

"Unlike you, I'm not going to pretend otherwise." Jess smiled again before pulling Allie along with her to catch up with Jared. Man, he had her interested.

I pushed open the door to one of my favorite bars. The Maple Leaf doesn't look particularly special on the outside, but the music and overall feel of the place made it worth coming back to. I headed straight through to the back patio, checking behind me to make sure Allie was still with me.

"Owen!" Hailey noticed us immediately and decided to annoy the hell out of Owen by pulling him into a hug.

I laughed to myself as he quickly broke away. "Aww, damn it, Hailey. I should have known you would be here."

"Don't bother hiding it, Owen. You know you're glad to see your favorite sister." She grinned.

"You mean my only sister."

Hailey quickly lost interest in Owen when she noticed the girls. "Hi. I don't think we've met." She held out her hand.

Allie accepted her handshake. "I'm Allie."

Hailey moved on to Jess next.

Hailey smiled at Jess before turning her attention to Allie again. "Nice to meet you. So you're friends with my brother then?"

Allie's brow furrowed slightly. "Sort of..."

"Enough of the twenty questions. We met them down at the hotel. Allie's dad owns the place now," Owen explained.

"Oh!" Hailey caught the glare I shot her and recovered quickly. Letting the girls know there was anything important about the hotel wouldn't be a good thing.

"Watch it, Hailey," Jared warned.

Hailey nodded at us both. She understood. "It's really nice to meet you both. My best friends deserted me to spend the summer abroad, and I could really use some other girls around."

"Wait, Beth and Jill both left already? Who are you here with?" Owen pretended not to care, but he was still her big brother.

"I came by myself to meet up with Jamie. Not a big deal."

"Oh, okay, but don't leave by yourself."

"Like I can't take care of myself?" She put a hand on her hip.

"Just humor me, Hailey."

"Sure." She rolled her eyes. "God, older brothers can be annoying. Do you have any siblings, Allie?"

"Nope, I'm an only child."

Interesting. It looked we had something in common.

"So lucky," Jess broke in. "I have four younger brothers and sisters."

"Four? Wow," Hailey was probably picturing having to deal with more than one Owen.

Jess nodded. "Yeah, I know. Thankfully, I was always able to escape the chaos by crashing at Allie's because her mom is cool. She's so lucky."

"My mom is pretty cool." Allie seemed to be lost in thought for a minute. I wondered what the story was. She'd mentioned her dad bought the hotel, but from what I knew, there wasn't a Mrs. around.

Satisfied she wasn't going anywhere, I slipped back inside to get us some drinks. There was a line at the bar, but the bartender served me immediately. I didn't know him by name, but he definitely knew who I was. I ordered myself an Abita and decided to go with another Oasis for Allie. She seemed to like the last two. I listened to the band for a few seconds before heading back outside. Allie was exactly where I left her.

"I got your drink for you." I held out her glass.

She seemed surprised. I guess she hadn't noticed my absence. "My drink?"

"You seemed to like it the other night."

"And you still aren't going to tell me what's in it?"

"Nope." No reason to reveal any of my cards yet.

"Well, there are other ways of figuring it out." She gave me a coy smile.

"Are there now?" Now this was good. Things were finally moving in the right direction.

"Uh-huh." Damn, a girl like that shouldn't be allowed to look at a man that way. My jeans weren't going to be my friend for long.

"You care to share?"

"Not right now." She smiled and took a seat next to Owen. I stifled the growl I felt rising in my throat. To make matters worse, Hailey jumped into the empty seat next to her before I got the chance. That girl was looking for trouble. I shot her a dirty look. Jess let out a giggle. She was perched on Jared's lap. He looked very pleased with the arrangement.

The table was also occupied by a few guys I knew from Society events. One of them immediately jumped out of his seat and offered it to me.

"That won't be necessary. I'm sure Allie and I can share." I looked right at her. If she was going to eye fuck me, I was going to do it right back.

"You wish."

"Why? You afraid you might actually like it?" I taunted. I was getting frustrated. She obviously wanted me too. Why was she being so difficult?

She shivered, and I loved that I had that effect on her. "Not a chance."

She stormed off inside. I gave her a few seconds head start before following her. She didn't notice. Instead, she got distracted by the music. I watched her body move to the beat, completely oblivious to anyone or anything around her. My body rebelled at the thought of her so unprotected. Where was this coming from? She was just a girl.

I ordered her another Oasis and waited until I saw her set aside her empty glass at the bar before approaching again. I leaned against the bar, waiting for her to notice. "I told you you'd like it here."

She turned to look up at me. "I admit it's pretty cool. Who is this, by the way?"

"Oh, it's the Rebirth Brass Band. Heard of them?"

"I don't think so, but that isn't surprising. I'm not exactly up on the New Orleans music scene. Anyway, what was that all about back there?"

"What do you mean?"

"Why do people act like you walk on water or something?"

"How do you know I don't?" I handed her the drink. She accepted it with a nod and took a long slow sip. My eyes went to her lips, so ready to know what they felt like. I was tired of waiting.

"Don't what?"

"Walk on water."

"Wow, you are even cockier than I thought."

I laughed. She really said what was on her mind.

"All right, I can't walk on water, but I can do other things very, very well." And I was ready to show her exactly what I meant.

"Oh yeah?" She licked her lip, and I knew she was thinking the same thoughts as me.

"Let me show you." I leaned in and brushed my lips against hers gently, just long enough for her to think I wasn't going to take it further. Without warning, I picked it up, crushing my lips into hers. She responded, and I wrapped her up in my arms, devouring the sweet taste of her mouth as her hands twisted in my hair. Every inch of me was on fire, begging for more. There was something special about her, and one kiss was definitely not going to be enough.

I heard someone clear their throat, bringing me back to where we were. I reluctantly broke the kiss. "Still going to pretend you aren't interested, Allison?"

She gazed up at me with this dazed expression. I laughed. "I told you to call me Allie."

"You said everyone calls you Allie. I'm not everyone." She wasn't going to be able to keep me at bay. Any chance of staying away from me was over the second my lips touched hers.

"Are you always this frustrating?"

"Depends on who you ask."

She groaned before setting aside her partially full glass. I followed her back out onto the patio. I was still on a high from the kiss and just trying to come up with the best way to ask her home. She wanted to, but I had the feeling she was still going to resist.

I sat watching her for hours. She seemed so comfortable hanging out with my friends, and she especially seemed to be hitting it off with Hailey. I liked that. Why? Why did I care if a girl I slept with was friends with my roommate's little sister? *Because I wanted her to stick around.* The thought hit me like a strike of lightning. Forget a few nights, I wanted this girl longer.

I zoned out most of their conversation, trying to keep my mind off the kiss and the growing bulge in my pants, by discussing college sports with Jared. Eventually, I got pulled back into their conversation. Somehow the topic of action movies had come up.

"Okay, so who would win in a fight, Jean-Claude Van Damme, Stephen Segal, Bruce Lee, or Jackie Chan?" Owen asked.

"Easy, Jean-Claude. I mean he's hot and bad ass. Can you get any better?" Allie answered animatedly.

"Wait, so I'm not the only 18-year-old Jean-Claude fan? Nice!" Hailey gave her a high five.

"That's who you find hot?" I smirked. "But anyway, Owen, you left out Chuck Norris."

"Please, no. Someone stop Levi from starting in on Chuck Norris. There are only so many of those jokes I can take." Hailey hit the table with her hand and spilled several of the drinks. For some reason, the girls thought this was funny, and they started cracking up. Allie had a great smile and an even better laugh.

"Wow, is it really 2:30?" She squinted at the face of her watch. She blinked a few times before pulling out a small bottle from her purse and putting in some eye drops. She must have had contacts. I couldn't relate. I had perfect vision.

"Did you guys drive?" Hailey asked.

"No, we took the streetcar." Allie yawned.

"Why don't you guys come back to our place? It's really late anyhow," Jared suggested.

"That sounds like a great idea." Jess ran her hand down Jared's leg.

Allie didn't hide her distaste at the idea. I tried not to let that irk me. "I'm sure it does, Jess."

"I'd have to agree." I smiled. She had to be messing with me. There was no way she wanted to go home.

"I'd invite you guys to crash at my house, but my parents will flip if they see that I've been drinking. I'm going to stay over at their place anyway," Hailey explained.

"You still live at home?" Allie seemed surprised.

"Yeah. I just graduated from high school."

"Oh, duh. You said you were eighteen. Okay, I'll stay at their place then." For some reason, knowing that Hailey was coming made the prospect more appealing to Allie. I'd have to remember to thank Hailey later.

CHAPTER SIX

"I knew I'd be taking you home tonight," I whispered as we walked toward our house. The night was warm, even at the late hour. There was no escaping the heat during the summer in New Orleans. Lucky for me, my body easily adjusted to any temperature. Unfortunately, that self-regulation didn't apply to the effect Allie had on me. One touch from her had me burning up.

She continued to play hard to get and shrugged my arm off her shoulder. I laughed. Now that I had the physical evidence of her interest, I wasn't as worried. That kiss had spoken volumes. She wanted me, and she wanted me bad.

I unlocked the front door, ushering Allie in before following closely behind her. She gazed around our living room as Jared led a giggling Jess down the hall to his room. Allie made a face when she noticed it out of the corner of her eye. She didn't try to stop her friend, but I sensed she wanted to. My guess is she was used to Jess' behavior. The girl wasn't drunk. Jared wasn't a complete asshole. We both had the same rule when it came to women. If they weren't sober enough to completely consent, then we let them go. There were plenty of girls to go around. Except I didn't feel that way that night. I didn't want anyone but Allie.

Allie seemed uptight. She took a seat on one of the leather couches, keeping her legs pressed firmly together. I wondered if the position was intentional, or if it was her subconscious attempt at resisting me. I sat down right next to her. I needed to put her at ease. She seemed most comfortable when I hit on her. I decided to go with it.

She blinked and yawned silently.

"You are more than welcome to sleep in my bed." I put my feet up on the circular ottoman.

"As tempting as that offer is, I'll take my chances out here." She took off her flip flops and curled her legs up on the couch under her. I fought the urge to pull her legs onto my lap. I'd have given her a foot rub if she'd wanted one. I'm definitely not a foot guy, but every part of Allie seemed worth exploring.

"Wow, Levi, you've never offered to let me take your bed before." Hailey feigned hurt.

"And I'll never offer you my bed. If you don't want to sleep on the couch, talk to your brother, or better yet, go home."

"Aww, you are always so sweet to me."

Allie laughed. My plan was working. She was relaxing. Owen took a seat on the couch across from us, and Hailey entertained Allie with stories of how much trouble we used to get into as kids. Before long, Allie's head slumped down on my shoulder.

Owen nodded to where she rested. "Looks like we bored her to death."

"Nah, she's just tired. Humans need more sleep than us." Hailey stretched.

"Are you going to wake her up?" Owen asked.

"No. I'll let her sleep." I ran a hand down her arm. She was so sweet all curled up that way against me. "Get me the extra quilt in my closet and you can take my room tonight, Hailey."

She stood up. "Where are you going to sleep?"

"Right here."

Owen laughed. "You've got it bad."

"She's comfortable, and besides, I don't want her to wake up confused about where she is."

"Sure. Tell yourself whatever it takes." Owen started toward his room. "Night, guys."

Hailey tossed the quilt down on the ottoman. "Be good, Levi. I like her."

"Yeah, so do I. Considering I'm giving up my room, I wouldn't worry."

"That's what worries me…"

I laughed. "Get out of here."

As Hailey disappeared down the hall, I kicked off my shoes and repositioned us so we were lying down together. I gave her body a long look before covering us both up with the quilt.

I cuddled her in my arms, trying to tune out the sounds of Jared and Jess down the hall. Normally, I'd be jealous he was getting some when I wasn't, but I wouldn't have traded places for anything. I'd never just lay down with a girl like that before, but I liked it. Her breathing was even, and the pattern of it relaxed me. I closed my eyes, leaning back into a throw pillow. I thought about our kiss, the taste of her, and how perfectly her body felt pressed against mine. The thought started to get me hard in the wrong place, so I tried to push it out of my head. There was no reason to get excited. Tonight wasn't the night, but it would happen.

Another image flashed through my mind. Another night, a fireplace and a skylight open to the stars. I forced my eyes open. I couldn't go there. That was a thought that could only hurt me. Still, there was something about this girl that got to me, and I knew it wasn't just about sex. If it was, I wouldn't have been so satisfied just holding her. I stayed awake for hours listening to her breathe. I relaxed completely, and I felt strangely comfortable considering the cramped space. Finally, my body protested to the late hour, and I kissed her cheek before drifting off to sleep.

***

My body was stiff, but I'd never woken up in such a good mood before. Allie was snuggled up flush against me, and her hair and hands were sprawled across my chest. I imagined how much better the morning would be if we weren't wearing clothes, but somehow I was okay with the current situation.

She stirred, quietly at first, before doing this adorable stretch with her arms. She seemed to notice the cramped space and opened her eyes.

"Good morning, beautiful."

She clutched the blanket against her. "Oh god."

"Sleep well?"

She blinked a few times and looked around. "What are you doing here?"

"You're in my apartment, or did you forget?" I liked saying that.

"I mean why are you sleeping on the couch with me? Why aren't you in your room?"

"Oh, I gave my bed to Hailey."

"But I thought you'd never..."

"I was just messing with her. Besides, I thought we could use the privacy." I couldn't resist egging her on.

"Was I really so zonked out I missed all of this?"

"You fell asleep in the middle of a conversation and were leaning against me. You looked too comfortable to disturb, so I just moved us a bit." I left out asking Hailey for a blanket. She didn't need to know I'd actually put thought into the arrangement.

"I see. Well, at least we're on the couch and not your bed."

"Don't sound so relieved about it." I tried to sound playful, but would it have been so bad if we'd spent the night in my room?

"Hmm, yeah, because it would have felt great to wake up in bed with a guy I don't know."

"You do know me, Allison." Her name felt like velvet on my tongue. I knew she didn't like it, but I liked the way it riled her up. Besides, I was serious about not calling her what everyone else did.

"That again?" She shifted around. I knew she was trying to get up, but I wasn't quite ready to let go yet.

"You are really cute when you get angry."

"Just shut up and let go of me so I can get the heck out of here."

"Wow, calm down. Aren't you going to let me make you breakfast? It's the least I can do for the girl I just spent the night with."

"I did not spend the night with you. We were on the couch." She blinked again. I'd have to make sure she brought a case for her contacts next time she spent the night at my place. The next time. That thought got me excited.

"You spent the night in my arms, sweetheart. Sex or no sex, you can't argue that."

She groaned just as Owen walked into the room. He always had impeccable timing. I moved my arm so Allie could sit up. She smoothed out her dress and stood.

"Good morning. Did you enjoy the wonderful accommodations of our living room?"

"Where's Jess? Please tell me she's here somewhere." Allie's voice was a mix of worry and embarrassment. She didn't need to feel either. Jared wouldn't have hurt Jess, and she'd slept with me on the couch. What was embarrassing about that?

"She's in with Jared," Owen and I answered at the same time.

"Um, could one of you please get her for me?" She picked up her purse off the ground and put back on her flip-flops. Was she really just going to leave like that?

I couldn't get upset about it. I had no reason to. I'd just take her out again and end the night in my bed next time. But maybe I could stall her awhile longer. "There's no way I'm taking the chance of seeing Jared naked." I stretched in an exaggerated way to let her know I wasn't in any hurry.

She scrunched up her face. "Gross. Fine. Which room is his?"

"Seriously?"

"Yes, seriously. We have to be at work in like twenty minutes."

Again about work? Maybe her dad was as much of a hard ass as mine. Even so, I still had to try to get her to stay awhile. "Well, if you are already going to be late, you might as well stay for breakfast."

"Which room is his?" She repeated.

Owen pointed and she marched down the hall. A few minutes later, she opened the front door with Jess chasing after her. She was busy fidgeting with her sandals as Allie stepped outside. "You could have at least let me get dressed!"

Allie didn't respond. She only threw her an annoyed look. Even her annoyed look was cute. I was losing it.

"Thanks for an amazing night, Allison!" I laughed, enjoying her reaction to everything. She was the cutest thing I'd ever seen. And the hottest.

The girls were still arguing as they stepped into a cab.

Jared walked out of his room in just a pair of pajama pants. "Lovely morning, isn't it?"

I ignored him and started to make a pot of coffee.

"What's gotten into him?" Jared hopped up on the island counter.

"He spent the night on the couch." Owen took a bite out of an apple.

"Wait? You gave up your room to the girl and didn't join her?" The huge smirk on Jared's face said it all.

"No. He spent the night on the couch with her."

"With clothes on?" Jared raised an eyebrow.

"Yes." I was tired of letting Owen answer for me.

Jared cracked up. "Seriously? You slept with the girl on the couch?"

"Her name's Allie." I may have called her Allison to her face, but I didn't want Jared calling her that too.

"Well, I definitely didn't just sleep on the couch with her friend."

"Yeah. We heard." Hailey walked into the kitchen.

"Too much for your innocent ears?" Jared smirked.

"Do you even remember her name?"

He laughed dryly. "It's Jess. Give me some credit."

"And do you know anything about her?" Hailey was really pushing her luck.

"Why do you care?" Jared hopped off the counter.

"Because you're better than that."

"Because I'm better than that?" He pointed to his chest. "What about her?"

"She can do whatever she wants. I'm worried about you. You're going to be heading for a lonely life if you don't stop this."

"Glad you're worried about me, but I'd be more worried about Levi here. I think he's lost his touch."

"Shut up," I snapped at him. I was frustrated enough already, although not about the lack of sex. Strangely, that didn't bother me. But she didn't stay. I refused to

45

believe she wasn't interested, but she was definitely making it hard.

"I'm proud of you," Hailey patted me on the shoulder.

"Great. Just what I always wanted."

"And I'm rooting for you. I like Allie and want her to stick around."

I poured myself a cup of black coffee. "She will be. Don't worry about that."

"What's your plan, Cassanova?" Owen reached around me to get a mug down from the cabinet.

"I'm taking her out for lunch."

"Funny. I didn't hear you guys making plans." Owen took a seat on a stool.

"We're going out to lunch." I made my exit. I was in no mood to listen to any more crap from my friends.

CHAPTER SEVEN

I wasn't positive what her job was at the hotel, but I knew someone who would undoubtedly know. I walked into the lobby and headed right over to the desk. Luck was with me, and the manager was standing behind one of the computers.

"Good afternoon, Natalie."

The blonde woman glanced up and her posture changed immediately. She stood up straight and plastered on a smile. "Good afternoon, Levi. What a pleasant surprise."

I smiled back. "I'm actually here to see Allie. We have lunch plans."

"Oh." A look of surprise crossed her face. "I didn't know you two were friendly."

I put a hand down on the counter between us. "We're more than friendly." I don't know why I added that part. I didn't have to. Natalie was going to tell me where Allie was no matter how well I knew her.

Natalie looked torn for a second. "She's in the back."

"Thanks for the assistance." I nodded before heading back around behind the desk.

Natalie nodded. "Of course."

I walked down the narrow corridor, peeking into each cubicle and office until I saw her. She was standing by the copy machine, sorting through a pile of papers.

I quietly made my way over to her. "Ready for lunch?"

Allie's mouth fell open. "What are you doing back here, Levi?"

"Oh, Natalie told me I could come back."

"Oh, did she?" Her face scrunched up the way it seemed to always do when she was getting heated.

"Yeah. You ready?"

"I'm not having lunch with you." She lowered her voice.

I wasn't going to do the same. I raised mine. "Well, you left without letting me make you breakfast this morning, so I thought I could at least take you to lunch."

The stares of everyone around us did the trick. She took hold of my arm, and we walked down the hall.

She stopped when we were out of view and earshot of everyone else. "I don't know what kind of game you're playing, but I'm not having it."

"What game? It's just lunch." I stood right next to her, fighting the urge to pull her into my arms.

"So, you just like humiliating me in front of the people I work with?"

"That humiliated you?" I'd been going for humor not embarrassment. And, well, I also wanted to make sure any male in the vicinity knew she was completely off limits.

"Of course it did!" she hissed. "Now they think I slept with you."

"And that's a problem because…" I let a small smile slip.

"Because this is my dad's hotel. Okay, Levi? My dad's. I don't need my dad hearing about this and thinking his daughter is some sort of slut."

"Being slutty would imply spending the night with lots of guys, not just one. Heck, you can even tell him I'm your boyfriend if it makes you feel better."

"My what?"

"Your boyfriend." Isn't that what girls wanted? They wanted people to think they were in a committed relationship. I didn't care what term she used as long as I got to see her again.

"Do you even know what that word means? Have you ever had a relationship that lasted more than a few days?"

"There is a first time for everything. Most girls would want to tame me." I was pushing it, but the expression of horror on her face was worth it. Allie's reactions were too much.

"Tame you? Oh my god, leave. Just leave, okay?"

"Not until you agree to go out with me."

She wrung her hands at her sides. "You have to be kidding me."

"Not at all. I have no place to be. I'm staying here until you agree."

"Why? What angle are you playing?"

"First you accuse me of playing games and now angles. You aren't very trusting, Allison." She was going to break. She wanted to give in, and she would.

"It's Allie! And you haven't given me a reason to trust you!"

"Let me." I ignored a few employees who were watching us while trying to act like they were doing something else.

"Okay."

Okay? Nice. "Dinner tonight? I'd say lunch but I'd rather give you time to cool down."

"Don't you ever give up?"

"Never. I'm not leaving until you say yes." I needed to see her again. I needed another chance.

She sighed. "Fine. Coffee Friday night. Then you leave me alone."

"I'll pick you up at 8:00 then."

"Sure, whatever. Now leave."

"I'll miss you too." I grinned. Mission accomplished.

***

"I think I should tell her." I sipped my beer, feeling old as we sat at the unofficial Tulane bar, The Boot. We didn't go in there much anymore, but I'd had business to discuss with one of the bouncers so we decided to stay for a while.

"Tell her?" Owen looked at me like I'd lost my mind. "I hope you're kidding."

"Why not tell her? Why wait?"

"And lose her before you even get a chance?"

"Don't be so overdramatic, man. Not every guy makes girls run from him." Jared took a jab at Owen's weak spot.

Owen moved his empty beer bottle around on the table. "Most girls would run from what we are. Why would Allie be any different?"

"I have a good feeling about her." I finished off my beer. "I think she's the one."

"You've only been out with her a few times. How would you even know?" Owen eyed me warily.

"Wait. As in *the* one?" Jared stopped checking out the girls at the next table long enough to comment.

"I don't know for sure, but there's only one way to find out."

"How could you possibly know that from sleeping on the couch with her? You're being crazy." Jared finished his beer and pushed the empty bottle away from him.

"Just make sure you know what you're doing." Owen watched me with concern. I understood. He'd met a girl freshman year and was ready to marry her after a few months. We all told him he was crazy, but he didn't listen. He let her in on the secret that we weren't human, and she went as far as transferring schools and changing her number to get away from him. He hadn't dated anyone since.

Owen wasn't me, and Allie wasn't that stupid girl. "This is different. This is real."

"Real?" Jared snorted. "It's because she's playing hard to get. Once you bag her, the feeling will pass."

"Shut up." I pounded my hand into the table, splitting the wood. "Okay. We need to go."

I nodded an apology at the bartender as I headed for the door. He knew we'd pick up the tab later.

"This is why you have to stay away from her." Jared caught up with me outside. "She's already screwing with your brain and you haven't even fucked her."

I felt my body tense, it wanted to transform. "Use a word like bagged or fuck in reference to Allie again and I'll rip you in two."

He held up his hands in front of him. "Chill out. Just think about it. Why are you getting so bent out of shape over her? She's just a girl."

"Maybe he actually likes her. Crazy concept, I know." Owen walked ahead of us.

"Just don't lose your head over a piece of ass. It's never worth it."

I resisted the urge to punch Jared. Piece of ass? Maybe when I first met her, but she was more than that now. Jared was right about one thing, she was screwing with my brain. But that didn't mean I was going to stay away from her. It meant I was going to do the opposite.

Chapter Eight

Natalie was quick to fill me in on Allie's room number when she never showed up in the lobby. I waited around for fifteen minutes before deciding to take matters into my own hands. Allie didn't seem like the type to stand someone up.

I listened outside her door for a minute, trying to determine whether she was alone. I didn't hear anything but a loud deep sigh. I was right that something was up with her. I knocked on the door.

She swung the door open quickly like she was expecting someone. Maybe she wanted me to come up and get her. We hadn't actually discussed where I was picking her up. She wore tight gym pants and a tank top without a bra. She looked hot, but she didn't look ready for a date.

"What are you doing here?"

She was blocking the doorway, so I walked around her. There was no reason to wait out in the hall. "Did you forget we had plans?"

"Plans? Oh, yeah, coffee, I forgot." She took a seat on the couch and pulled her knees up to her chest.

I knelt down in front of her and made complete eye contact. I felt a pang in my chest as I thought about someone hurting her. "Hey, what's going on, Allie?"

"You're calling me Allie?"

"Whoa, now you're annoyed at me for calling you Allie? Can a guy ever get a break?" I tried to keep myself calm, but she didn't look like herself.

She shrugged.

"Seriously, are you okay?"

"I guess, but this summer has turned into a disaster." She exhaled loudly. "Jess left and my dad still hasn't come back. So yeah, great, I get to spend the rest of the summer all alone. Just what I needed."

I rested a hand next to her on the couch. "Hey, don't say you're alone. Don't I count for something?"

She smiled, and a weight lifted. "That's what I was looking for. It's going to be okay. But why did Jess leave?"

"It's—" She stopped suddenly. "It's personal."

My gut told me it was about Jared, but I decided to leave it. There was no reason to make her talk about something she didn't want to. "I'll take that, but on one condition."

"What?"

"Come out with me tonight. I promise I'll cheer you up."

She hesitated, and for a second I worried she'd say no. "Sure, just let me get changed."

She'd just walked into her bedroom when I heard another knock. Who else would be coming to her room? I pulled open the door, ready to defend my territory, but I quickly relaxed. It was just room service.

"Just leave it. Here you go." I handed the guy a ten, accepted the tray, and closed the door.

I opened the Styrofoam container and found a large slice of carrot cake complete with the little sugar carrot on top. "You want to eat cake first, or do you want to get changed?"

"I'm not in the mood for it anymore. You can have it or just put it in the fridge."

She disappeared into the bathroom, and I moved the cake from its container onto a plate before putting it in the fridge. I figured it would be a nice surprise for her later that night, or maybe the next morning, depending on when she came home.

I walked around the suite, noting how clean and orderly it was. Allie was either a neat freak or super organized. I was neither, but I wasn't a slob. I picked up the e-reader she must have discarded when I came in. I read a few paragraphs and it was either a romance or chic lit or something. The choice surprised me. I would have expected her to be reading something more literary.

I was about ready to turn on the TV when her cell phone rang. Curious when I saw a guy's name flash across the screen, I picked it up. "Hello?"

I heard a sound of something dropping. Allie must have heard me answer. I smiled to myself.

"Who is this? Is Allie there?" An angry male voice yelled at me from the phone.

"No, Allie's not available right now. She's getting changed." Both true statements.

"Who the hell are you?"

"Who am I? The name's Levi." I laughed to myself. This was kind of fun.

"Tell Allie Toby's on the phone. Her boyfriend Toby."

"Well, hello Toby, but I'm sorry I think Allie would have mentioned a boyfriend before she spent the night at my place. Are you sure you don't mean ex-boyfriend?" Jess had specifically said she'd sworn off men, so she definitely didn't have a boyfriend. Either this guy was delusional or he was just so hung up on her he couldn't accept she'd moved on. I heard her breathing from just inside the door. She hadn't come out to stop me. Another interesting observation.

"Go to hell, asshole."

"No, I won't go to hell, but I'll take a message." I laughed out loud this time. The call disconnected. "You can come out now. I'm off."

She opened the door slowly. "How'd you know I was listening?"

"I heard you breathing."

"You heard me through the door?" She sounded skeptical.

"You didn't really think you were fooling me, did you?" Like she couldn't hear every word I said.

"Whatever. I can't believe you answered my phone."

"You could have stopped me at any time. Something tells me you have no problem with what I told Toby." She liked it. She liked that I handled the ex for her. That was a good start.

"You're right."

"I'm sure I am, but about what exactly?"

"That I don't mind what you said. He's my ex-boyfriend. We broke up a few months ago and he hasn't really accepted it."

Bingo. The situation was easy to read. "I can't say I blame him." I took her in. She'd changed into a new tank top, this time with a bra underneath, and a pair of tight dark jeans. Not quite as nice as a short skirt, but when she turned around, I decided the rear view more than made up for it.

"So, aren't we going out?" She watched me.

"Yes, the night awaits." I held open the door, and we walked out into the hallway. This was our first time going out just the two of us, and anyway you spun it, she was letting me take her out on a date.

Chapter Nine

I picked a coffee shop right down the block from the hotel. I went generic, just wanting a quiet place to sit and talk for a while. She was still bummed about her friend leaving, and I needed to change that. We'd start with coffee and then take things from there.

I led her over to an empty table. "What can I get you?"

"Oh. Just a coffee."

"Room for cream?" She didn't strike me as a black coffee kind of girl, but then again, she didn't strike me as one who read romance books either.

"Nope. I like Splenda in it though."

"Okay." I smiled before going over to the counter to get our drinks. I returned to the table with the coffees. I'd already stirred a sweetener packet in hers. She took a sip before reaching over to grab a second packet of sweetener from the plastic dish.

I watched her carefully stir the hot coffee. "Two?"

"I like things sweet."

I bet she did. The words "do you like things hard too?" swirled through my head, but I wisely kept them to myself. She might like my flirting, but that kind of comment would probably get me a slap in the face.

"What really brought you down here this summer?" I'd been trying to figure it out all week. Something wasn't adding up.

"What do you mean? Working at the hotel…"

"That's what you say, but couldn't you have gotten a job back home?" Was it all about that Toby guy? Was she running from him?

"What does it matter?"

"I'm just trying to figure you out."

"Figure me out?" She leaned forward slightly.

"You have to be the hardest girl to read."

She laughed. "I can't be that hard to read."

I laid it all out there. "We have a girl with a few months before leaving for college and instead of staying home to enjoy time with her friends, either bumming around or working some silly part time job, you drive across the country to work at a hotel for a dad who has been here all of one day since you arrived."

"Get to the point." She eyed me suspiciously.

"Either this is all an elaborate effort to get away from your ex, or you're running from something else."

She crossed her arms over her chest. "I'm not running from anything."

Defensive mannerism. I was getting close. "So it's all Toby?"

"No, it's not."

"Okay, so what is it?" Something in me needed to know. I needed to know what made this beautiful, infuriating woman tick.

"Can't there be a third choice? I wanted to try something new."

"Isn't college trying something new already?" It was definitely a big change from high school, especially if you went away from home.

"Yes, but that's different."

"Different?" I sipped my coffee.

"Yeah, I don't know, it just seemed like an adventure."

"An adventure? You're looking for an adventure, huh? Where do I sign up?" I wriggled an eyebrow at her. Now we were talking. If she wanted adventure, she'd come to the right place. Owen's warning words flooded my head, but I ignored them. This felt right. I was showing her my true self. If she wanted to run, she might as well get it over with before I fell harder. Was that possible? Was it possible to want a girl more than I already wanted her?

She laughed. "Stop. I just mean no one would ever expect me to spend a summer in New Orleans. It's different and it was so last minute. I actually quit another job at the last second so I could come here."

I feigned shock. "What? How could you?"

"Well, I guess it wasn't quitting because I didn't quite start, but I was supposed to be a lifeguard at a local beach. I changed my mind when my dad called to invite me down."

"Then I propose a toast." I lifted my cup.

"A toast? With coffee?"

"You can toast with any beverage."

"Sure, why not?" She raised her cup. "But what are we toasting?"

"To Allie's great adventure."

She laughed again as our cups touched and her eyes finally got that twinkle back. I put my cup to my lips and drank the last of my coffee like I was taking a shot. That got her smiling.

Her phone rang. I hoped it wasn't that Toby kid again.

"It's Jess. Do you mind if I get this?"

"No, not a problem." Jess I could handle. Besides, maybe if they talked, Allie would feel better about things. I wanted her in a good mood for the rest of the night.

She answered. "Hey, are you home?"

I listened in to the other end of the conversation. I couldn't catch every word, but I caught enough. *"Yeah, I got in about ten minutes ago. I wanted to apologize."*

"It's okay. I completely understand."

Allie glanced at the door. Another group of customers poured in. They were a rowdy bunch of tourists wearing beads they must have purchased at a store. Why people would spend money on those crappy pieces of plastic I'd never understood.

"Hey, where are you?" Jess must have heard the crowd.

"Out getting coffee." Allie smiled.

"With who?"

"Umm, can I call you later?" She looked down at the table.

Allie pushed the phone tighter against her ear. I tried to hear but the only thing I caught was my name.

She played with her coffee cup. "Maybe."

I stopped trying to listen. I'd heard what I needed to. She disconnected and sat up enough to slide her phone in her back pocket. I realized she hadn't brought a purse with her that night.

"Jess made it back?" I decided to pretend I hadn't heard the conversation for myself.

"Yeah, she just got home."

"Anything else going on?"

"Nope."

"Exciting."

She flipped her hair back. "Isn't it?"

"How's the coffee?" I made conversation but really I was planning things out in my head. If I was ready to reveal myself, I had to show her. Telling her would probably just leave her thinking I was crazy or just making it up as a joke. Showing her would be easy enough, but how was I going to handle the fall out if she didn't take it well? Should I give her some space to think about it, or force her to face it head on? I'd be willing to give her space, although I really hoped she'd shock me and accept what I was without a problem. It was a delusional thought, but I clung to it.

We talked about traveling and other random stuff for a while, and it was only a little before nine thirty when she finished her coffee. She set down her empty cup. "This was actually fun. Thanks, I needed it."

"My pleasure. See, giving me a chance wasn't so bad, was it?"

"Hey, don't read too much into it. We had coffee. End of story."

"Does it have to be the end?" I looked her straight in the eye.

"What else do you have in mind?"

"Want to meet up with my friends? I bet Hailey will come if she knows you are. I think she has a girl crush on you." Hailey had asked about her at least five times that week. She'd even texted me. That had given Jared a laugh and Owen a heart attack. He was always afraid Hailey would push me too far. I didn't care.

"A girl crush? What are you, like three?"

"No… it's just funny. She talks about you almost as much as I do." Had I said that out loud? I guess telling her I talked about her wasn't necessarily a bad thing. She already knew how I felt.

"I think she's pretty cool too. Definitely different from my other friends."

"Different is good, right?" If she liked different, I might be okay.

"It can be."

"Are you up for hanging out more?" I asked it as a question, but I wasn't taking no for an answer. Now that I'd built up the anticipation, I couldn't back down.

"Yeah, okay."

I led her through the French Quarter, watching her reaction to everything. She might be used to city life, but New Orleans was something altogether different. Although touristy, the Quarter was still a special place, and I was glad she seemed interested in it. If things were going to work between us, she'd have to start calling New Orleans home. Leaving wasn't an option for me. I was crown prince, and the throne was in the basement of the Crescent City Hotel.

She stopped short in front of a dark bar on the corner. I smiled when I saw what got her attention.

"Wow, are those people seriously dressed up as vampires?" Her eyes were glued on a couple of humans who were holding up a chalice and pretending to drink blood.

I laughed. "If you think those people are weird, you'd be freaked out by the real thing."

"The real thing? Very funny." She started walking again.

"What, you don't think vampires are real?" Here it was. How much did she believe in the legends already?

"No, and I'm glad they aren't."

"Why? Do they scare you?" I stopped and took her arm so I could turn her to look at me.

"Does the thought of blood sucking monsters scare me? Hell yes. Who wouldn't be scared of that?"

I laughed again. Allie was in for one hell of a surprise. "Trust me, sweetheart, in New Orleans, vampires are the least of your worries."

"What do you mean?"

"I'm really glad you asked that."

Her face paled slightly. "What are you talking about?"

"You'll have to wait and see."

"Okay, listen, scaring me isn't a good way to get me interested, so if you have any weird tricks up your sleeve. just shelve them." She balled her hands into fists. I could tell it wasn't anger, but nerves that prompted the action.

"No tricks, hon." I pulled out my phone and texted Owen. It was still early, but I hoped they'd made it downtown already. The plan was to meet them on my own if things didn't go anywhere with Allie and to bring her if they did. The part of the plan they didn't know yet was that I wasn't waiting.

You there yet?

Yeah. Hailey tagged along too. Is it just you?

No. We're both coming.

Cool.

I'm doing it. There, I'd said it.

You're crazy.

Don't act surprised.

I pocketed my phone. "We're meeting everyone over at Club 360."

"What's that?"

"The lounge on the top of the World Trade Center down by the river."

"Okay, is it a cool view?"

"Yeah, it's got a good view." I laughed again. She had no idea how good of a view she was about to see.

"You promise you aren't luring me into some trap?"

"A trap? No. Let's just call it a new experience." The first wave of nerves hit me. Was I really doing this? Was I really taking the chance? Yes. There was no backing down.

We walked in a comfortable silence, and I held open the door when we arrived. There was a short wait for an elevator, but it was empty when we stepped in. I watched her, trying to hide my nerves.

The elevator doors opened on the top floor, dumping us out right at the club. I led her through the crowd, noticing that she kept checking out her outfit.

"Don't worry, we won't be here long." Not that she had to care about being underdressed.

"Why are we here at all then?"

"Do you ever stop asking questions?" To handle my nerves, I decided to give her a hard time. That usually worked for both of us.

"I only ask this many questions when I fear for my well-being."

"I assure you that you are in good hands." I put an arm around her waist, needing her close to me. Her touch reminded me of how important this was. I needed her to know what I really was. She had to accept I wasn't human, and hopefully she'd like the perks that came with it. I had more to offer her than she could imagine. I spotted my friends. "I see them."

The three of them were seated at a small window table. Only Jared had a drink. Owen and Hailey were looking around the room nervously.

"Allie! I'm so glad you came!" Hailey jumped out of her seat and hugged her. Allie beamed. It seems that the girl crush went both ways.

Allie smoothed out her tank top, bringing my attention to her stomach. I was sure it was toned and smooth. Picturing her skin helped relax me. "Yeah, I needed a night out."

"Where's your friend?" Jared asked casually.

"My friend? You mean Jess? She's back in New York, thanks to you."

I was right. It was about Jared.

Jared gave me a confused look. "She left? What does that have to do with me?"

"Nothing. Forget I said anything." Allie slipped into the empty seat next to Hailey.

"Okay..." Jared shrugged.

She gazed out the window, and once again, I wanted to know what she was thinking. Was she still upset about Jess? Was she just enjoying the view? The only view I cared about was her.

My friends watched me carefully. They were trying to see if I was going to chicken out. I still could. I could just ask Allie to dance and then take her home. Theoretically, I could just do it another night, but I wasn't a quitter. Just like I wasn't giving up on getting her, I wasn't backing down on my plans. Hailey asked me the silent question, and I nodded.

"All right, are you guys ready to go?" Hailey asked.

Allie turned away from the window. "What, already? I haven't even had a chance to enjoy the view."

I leaned over close to her. "You think this is a good view? Oh, just you wait."

"What are you talking about?"

"You sure about this, Levi? You know there is no turning back, right?" Owen looked at me, trying to avoid catching Allie's eye.

"Absolutely." I smiled.

Jared pushed out his chair. "Well, then, let's get going. It's supposed to rain later tonight."

"Why does the rain matter?" Allie's face appeared to be a mix of nerves and excitement. I really hoped the excitement won over.

"Are you ready to find out just how far the rabbit hole goes, sweetheart?" I reached out a hand to her. She needed to come with me willingly.

"Rabbit hole?" She seemed to hesitate. "Umm, sure?"

She put her hand in my mine. I led her through the crowd, and past the elevators. Jared took the lead, and we walked into the stairwell. She turned to look at me once more before starting up the stairs.

We were about halfway up when she finally questioned our destination. "Okay, why are we going to the roof?"

She was frightened, and I wanted to fix everything for her. The problem was I couldn't give her any easy answers. "No more questions." I tried to calm both of us.

"But—"

I gently pressed the palm of my hand into her back, hoping it had an effect on her. Touching her in anyway set me simultaneously on fire and put me at ease. "No more questions."

"It's all right. We're not taking you up there to kill you." Hailey laughed. Great. Because that didn't sound creepy.

Allie let out a deep breath. "Fine."

We walked up the remaining stairs and into the muggy night. The lights of the city reflected off the water. This was it. No turning back. I used her moment of distraction to pull off my shirt. My friends did the same. Hailey pulled off her sweater so she was just in a tank top.

I moved behind Allie and wrapped my arms around her waist.

She struggled against me so I loosened my hold. I let out a slow deep breath.

"What the hell..." she trailed off as she backed away from me. Her eyes widened.

I tried to keep my voice as soothing as possible. "Now don't freak out. I promised you I wouldn't hurt you, and I always keep my promises."

"Are you guys in a cult or something? Because if you are, I'm really not interested. I won't tell anyone anything, but if you don't mind, I'm leaving." She crossed her arms protectively.

"Chill out!" Jared yelled as his eyes changed to black. He was already transforming. He was the one who needed to stay calm.

I glared at him. "Don't talk to her like that."

He nodded, understanding the warning in my command. His eyes slowly returned to normal.

Hailey took a few steps toward Allie. I let her. Maybe a female would put her more at ease. "We're not a cult. It's more like a very special society." That was probably a good way to put it.

"A special society?" Allie's thoughts were clear on her face. She thought we were high or psychotic.

"Maybe it would be better if we just showed her." Owen smiled at her, and I appreciated him trying to help even though I knew he didn't support my decision. "You were sure you wanted this Levi, so there is no turning back."

He walked over to the edge of the building and raised a hand in a small wave before taking a backwards step and disappearing from sight.

"Oh my god! What the hell? Did he just kill himself?" Allie started shaking and crying. I wanted to reach out for her, but I wanted to let everyone go first.

"Owen's fine," Hailey said before jumping off with Jared right behind her.

Allie closed her eyes. I moved behind her again and wrapped her up in my arms. Her warm body fit perfectly against my bare chest.

"You said you wanted an adventure." I tightened my hold.

I let myself transform, reveling in the familiar feel of my large black wings extending from my back. I felt a wave of strength roll over me as I prepared to jump. I'd never flown with someone in my arms before, and Allie wasn't just anyone. She was everyone.

I stepped off.

I could tell she still had her eyes closed. Her body was so tense. She needed to see that everything was going to be okay. "Open your eyes," I whispered.

She let out the tiniest start of a scream before going silent. I continued our decent and then leveled us out just above the water. Part one was over. If she accepted me, wings and all, I may have found my mate. If she didn't, I wasn't sure what I was going to do. In the deepest part of my heart and soul, I knew there was no one else for me.

Follow Allie and Levi's story in the Crescent Chronicles. All three books are available now! The Pteron story then continues in the Empire Chronicles. Keep reading for a preview of Flight (the crescent chronicles #1) and Soar (the empire chronicles #1).

For more information about Alyssa Rose Ivy's books, please visit her online at:

www.AlyssaRoseIvy.com
www.facebook.com/AlyssaRoseIvy
Twitter.com @AlyssaRoseIvy
AlyssaRoseIvy@gmail.com

To stay up to date on Alyssa's new releases, join her mailing list: http://eepurl.com/ktlSj

FLIGHT

THE CRESCENT CHRONICLES

ALYSSA ROSE IVY

PREFACE

Closing my eyes, I tried to block it all out. Convinced I was about to die, I was only partly aware of his arms around me.

"You said you wanted an adventure," he said quietly, teasingly, as he tightened his hold.

My stomach dropped out as an intense and complete feeling of weightlessness engulfed me. The wind stung my face as memories flooded my mind. I thought of my parents, of all the things I wanted to tell them but never did, my friends from home, and the experiences I longed for. Quickly my thoughts changed to more recent memories, to Levi.

"Open your eyes," he whispered, somehow knowing my eyes were clenched shut.

Against my better judgment, I listened. The scream died in my throat as we hurtled toward the water that had seemed so beautiful from the roof above.

CHAPTER ONE

I'd sworn off men, or really boys, because those were
the only type of males I tended to attract. The numbers
on the pump moved painfully slow as I reminded myself
of the decision. Tying my hair up in a knot on the top of
my head, I struggled to save my neck from the heat
created by my long brown hair. Even a ponytail wasn't
enough for the Mississippi heat. I had heard all about the
hot summers of the south, but I didn't expect the
temperatures to be quite so scorching in June. I was
terrified to think about what August would feel like.

Finally finished with the gas, I got back in the car to
wait impatiently for my best friend Jess. We were only a
few hours away from New Orleans, but after two days of
driving, every minute was torture. I started the engine
and turned the AC on high before leaning back into the
comfortable seat. The new car smell still permeated my
Land Rover, an over the top high school graduation gift
from my father. I loved it and appreciated the gift but
wished my dad had checked with me before special
ordering it in what he believed was my favorite color—

lavender. I didn't have the heart to tell him that purple had stopped being my favorite when I was five.

After a few minutes, Jess slid into the passenger seat. "Want some chips or soda?" she asked while smoothing out her blond hair, putting a few strands back in place behind her ear. The effort was wasted. Her hair was still messy and matched the flushed expression she wore.

"Please tell me you didn't make out with someone to get free chips." I rolled my eyes hoping she would surprise me just this once by not having done it. We had been best friends since the sixth grade, and she had been boy crazy the whole time I'd known her.

"I didn't make out with him for the chips; I did it because he was hot."

Stifling a laugh, I pulled back out onto the road toward I-59. "Sure."

"We're only young once. Don't be so uptight." Jess snapped her gum loudly.

"Hey, it's fine, but don't come complaining to me when you get some weird communicable disease from one of the random guys you hook up with."

"Allie, I love you, but you have to relax. Promise me you'll at least try to have fun this summer." She sighed dramatically.

"I'll try," I said with exaggerated frustration. I planned to have a great summer, just one that didn't involve guys.

"That's not good enough. You're not going to let Toby ruin the entire summer are you? So you dated a jerk, who cares, forget about him."

"I'm not going to let Toby ruin anything. I'm the one who dumped him, remember?" Thinking about Toby threatened to put me in a worse mood. He had only been the latest in a string of disappointing dating experiences. First there was Steve, we broke up when I found him cheating on me—with my best guy friend. After that was

Matthew, who took commitment phobia to a whole new level when he actually set a cap on how often I could text message him. With Toby it wasn't anything dramatic, the romance just didn't live up to my expectations. Somehow, his declarations of how great of a power couple we would make didn't cut it. As relieved as I was about avoiding him all summer, I still had to deal with him at Princeton in the fall.

"So does that mean you're ready to move on?" Jess asked excitedly.

"No. I told you, I've sworn off men."

"Sweetheart, you do realize that men have many valuable roles other than boyfriends, right? Instead, how about you swear off boyfriends and just have fun?"

"I don't care what you do with guys, but I am never going to be the girl that just hooks up, okay?"

"We'll see about that."

Wanting to avoid a fight, I decided to ignore her last comment. Sometimes it was easier to let her think she won.

When I didn't answer, she decided to continue. "Maybe getting away from high school boys will help."

"Maybe," I mumbled under my breath.

She appeared not to hear me and changed the subject. "It was so cool of your dad to let us come down and hang out at the hotel all summer!"

"You mean it was cool of him to give us jobs, right?" I tried to keep a straight face, but really, I wasn't surprised by her choice of words. When Dad called to ask if I wanted to work at a hotel he had recently purchased in New Orleans, I agreed only if Jess could come with me. She wouldn't be much use as a coworker but she did have the ability to make any situation fun. I was counting on her working her magic.

***

The Crescent City Hotel looked exactly as I expected; a historic building complete with wrought iron balconies and the dangling ferns that were in every picture I had seen of the French Quarter. Following along with the GPS, I turned onto Royal Street and pulled up front to the valet, not sure where I was supposed to park. Before I could worry for long, my dad knocked on the window.

He opened the door once I unlocked it, taking my hand to help me out. "Hey sweetie, how was the trip?" He pulled me into a hug as soon as my feet hit the pavement. If you didn't know any better you'd think we had a normal father-daughter relationship.

"It was fine, we made great time."

"Hi Mr. Davis!" Jess yelled as she ran around the car.

"Hi Jessica, I'm so glad you were able to come down with my Allie."

"Of course! Thanks again for the job!"

"It's my pleasure; I hope you girls have a nice time." He caught my eye over Jess's head. Even as little as he knew Jess, he was under no misconceptions about her work ethic.

Dad glanced behind him, lifting a finger and a bellhop a little older than us started unloading bags from the back of the car. Before he had finished moving our bags to the cart, Jess was already chatting him up. With my dad watching, the poor guy was trying to stay professional.

"Let's go Jess." I grabbed her arm and led her inside. Dad had already gone ahead.

The lobby felt huge, much larger than it looked from the outside. All the money my dad had poured into the updates showed. Large travertine tiles covered the floor and dark wainscoting framed the room, while a beautiful chandelier with dangling crystals helped light the space. The etched glass in the sidewall that bore the name of the hotel typified the way he had modernized the hotel without losing all its historical character. I especially loved the solid mahogany bar. I'd like to say my dad had an eye for design, but I'm sure he had nothing to do with the selections. The fact that he was even at the hotel was surprising. He usually oversaw his properties from afar.

Looking up from the bar, I locked eyes with an incredibly hot guy. At over six feet tall with brown hair and wearing a tight shirt that barely concealed his muscular arms and chest, it would have been impossible not to notice him. He smiled at me and I found myself smiling back before I snapped myself out of it. Ignoring the invitation in his smile I quickly looked away. "You swore off men," I reminded myself.

"Do you girls want to see your room or get some lunch first?" my dad asked, relieving me of my thoughts about the guy.

"See our room," I answered quickly. "Is that okay, Jess?"

"Yeah, sure," she said distantly. I didn't bother looking, assuming she had found the same distraction.

My dad laughed as he led us to the elevators. "I put you girls in a suite on the top floor."

The elevator reached our floor and we walked toward our room. It came as no surprise, but our suite was luxurious. Jess and I each had our own room with a bathroom and we shared a large common living space complete with a kitchenette. Two French doors in the main living area opened out onto a balcony overlooking the street below.

"Wow Dad, you really didn't need to give us this suite for the whole summer."

"Of course I did. I'm your father. Now, why don't you girls get yourself settled and meet me in the courtyard for lunch in about a half hour?"

"Sounds great," I answered.

As soon as the door clicked Jess gave me a knowing smile. "So, uh, I thought you were swearing off guys."

"I am," I said defensively. Damn, she must have caught me eyeing him.

"Don't try to deny it. I saw you checking out that guy and he was checking you out too by the way. Totally hot, but I'll let you have him, his other friends were cute too."

"Don't even start." My response was automatic but inside I was surprised I hadn't even noticed his friends.

"Oh, come on, promise me that if he's still there you'll go talk to him," Jess pushed.

"No way."

"Why not?" she asked.

"Because I'm not interested, end of story."

"Oh no, you aren't getting off that easily."

Thankfully, I was saved from further argument by a knock. The bellboy from outside had arrived with our bags. He unloaded them two at a time, leaving them just inside the door.

"Do you girls need anything else?" Without my dad's presence he seemed much more interested in talking.

"I think we're all set for now, but we might need something later." Jess had turned on the charm.

"Oh yeah? Maybe I should give you my number then. I'm Billy by the way."

I tuned out their conversation, grabbing one of my bags to move it into my bedroom. Shaking my head, I laughed. I had to admit the bellboy was cute; he had the blond surfer boy look going for him, but leave it to Jess to get a phone number a few minutes after arriving in a city.

I heard the door click closed moments before Jess bounded into my room.

"Oh my god, this is going to be an awesome summer." She sprawled out on my bed.

"Hey Jess?"

"Yeah?"

"Don't ever change, okay?" I laughed.

"Are you making fun of me?" She sat up indignantly.

"Not at all. I just know I'm going to miss you this year."

"Aww, I'll miss you too. But we'll only be a train ride apart." She was going to her dream school, NYU.

"I know."

"And you could have gone to school in the city. You're the one who wanted to head to Jersey."

"Yeah, because Princeton is really settling, huh?"

"It is when you are only going there because your parents want you to."

I brushed it off, unwilling to let her know how much the jab hurt. "Let's go meet my dad; I'm starving." I headed to the door before Jess could argue. I'd never told her how I'd actually wanted to go somewhere more urban for school. Either she was more perceptive than I thought, or I was more transparent.

My eyes drifted to the bar as we walked through the lobby to the restaurant. I sighed with relief, but couldn't help but feel some disappointment as I noticed the now empty bar area.

"I guess you're off the hook for now, but next time you won't be so lucky," Jess said as she noticed the expression on my face.

I didn't even answer.

Flight **is available now!**

SOAR

THE
EMPIRE CHRONICLES

ALYSSA ROSE IVY

CHAPTER ONE
CASEY

Glowing Eyes. In the chaos of the moment, the only thing I could focus on were the yellow eyes that followed my every move. They were eerie and seemed more at home on an animatronic creation than on the living, breathing animal that had me cornered in the alley. I knew I was stuck, but I didn't think about death. It wasn't an option because I wasn't ready for it. Realistic or not, I was a firm believer that we make our own destiny.

I stepped back, convinced that if I walked backward slowly enough, I'd escape. I silently cursed Eric for making me throw out the trash after my shift. He was such an ass of an assistant manager.

At first, the wolf didn't move—at least I thought it was a wolf, although it seemed two sizes too big. As strange as it should have been to see a giant wolf in an alley, I'd seen far stranger in my nine months of living in New York City.

"Easy boy," I said in a half whisper, more for myself than for the beast now taking slow, deliberate steps toward me.

All of a sudden, he lunged. Gray fur moved in a blur as I blocked my face the best I could in the spilt second I had. A whimper rang out, and I lowered my arms when the contact never came.

The gray wolf slowly limped out of the alley. I searched for an explanation as I struggled to regain my breath and vaguely saw another figure disappear into the distance. He could have been any man, except that in my adrenaline-rich state, I could have sworn he had wings.

My head started to spin, and I reached out for something to hold onto. Then everything went black.

***

"Hey, Bates! Are you okay?"

I forced my eyes open, confused about the cause of my killer headache and the fogginess permeating my head.

"Casey?" Eric bent down next to me with some legitimate concern on his face. "Are you all right?"

"How long have I been out here?" I glanced around, trying to make sense of how I ended up face down in a pile of trash outside my place of work.

"Not too long. When you never came in from tossing the trash I got worried."

Likely. Eric was probably more worried about being named in a potential law suit.

"I'm fine... I think." I struggled to remember what had happened. The only memory I had couldn't be real. It involved a wolf and a strange guy with wings. Evidently I managed to pass out and hit my head on a trash can. Because that's normal.

"Are you sure? Do you think you can walk?"

"Yeah, I can walk." The alternative was to let him carry me inside. Despite his good looks, Eric's personality nullified any desire to have him hold me, even if walking seemed like an insurmountable task at the moment. Out of necessity, I accepted his outstretched hand and leaned heavily on his shoulder. My head continued to throb, and all I wanted to do was get home and lie down.

He put me down on the couch in the break room. The worn sofa wasn't a place I ever wanted to lay my head, considering it was twenty years old and had probably never been cleaned, but I didn't have a choice. The world was spinning.

"Did you hit your head?" Eric asked, taking a seat next to me. His muscular arm blocked my view of the room.

I reached up and touched the knot forming on the back of my head. "Yes. I have no idea how."

"Only you would do something that ridiculous." He routinely made fun of me, but something was off. Then again, I'd hit my head so maybe everything was off.

"Can you get my purse? It's in that locker." I pointed around him to where I'd stowed my stuff.

"Sure." He walked across the room and retrieved my ancient knock-off Gucci. He handed it to me, and I fished out my phone.

"Are you calling someone to get you?" He settled in next to me. The couch sunk down from the extra weight.

"Yeah. My cousin." I hit Rhett's name on my contacts list.

"Casey?" Rhett answered after two rings. Five years older than me, Rhett and I didn't hang out much, but he was being seriously awesome by letting me crash in the spare bedroom (read closet) in his apartment in the Village.

"Any chance you could walk down to Coffee Heaven?"

"Sure...but is there a particular reason why?" He sounded distracted, which probably meant he was buried in his research. A twinge of guilt went through me when I thought about bothering him, but asking Eric to walk me home was out of the question, and we were the only two closing.

"I kind of passed out and hit my head."

"What?" Shuffling, followed by a door slamming, let me know he was on his way. I worked a few blocks from Rhett's place, so I knew it wouldn't be long. "Hold tight. I'll be right there."

"I could have walked you home." Eric stood up, probably getting ready to unlock the front door for Rhett. He opened his mouth like he wanted to say more, but he quickly shut it.

"Rhett doesn't mind."

Eric mumbled something incomprehensible before stomping off through the doorway. I didn't really get him. He was a jerk to me most of the time, but then other times he got almost protective.

Eric returned minutes later with Rhett on his heels.

"You okay, Case?" Rhett kneeled down in front of me. As usual, his brown hair was all rumpled, and it looked like he hadn't showered yet. It was ten o'clock at night.

"I think so."

"What happened to her?" He looked at Eric, an unspoken accusation hanging in the air.

"I'm not positive. She went out to toss the trash and when I came out to look for her, she was on the ground."

"Next time, throw out the trash yourself." Rhett helped me up. "Casey won't be coming in to work tomorrow."

"Hey. I will so. I need the shift." My savings were dwindling, and that didn't bode well for going back to school the next semester.

Rhett shook his head. "No, you don't."

"I do. Eric, don't find someone to cover me. I'll be in."

"See you tomorrow, Bates." Eric blatantly ignored my cousin and called me by my last name. No matter how many times I reminded him that I preferred he use my first name, he disregarded the request.

"Night," I called just before the door closed behind us, leaving us in the brisk night air.

"You're a glutton for punishment, kid."

"Who are you calling kid?" I linked my arm with Rhett's as we walked past Washington Square Park. I was feeling better but was still light headed.

"You're nineteen. You're a kid."

"I don't feel like one." Working full time and trying to support myself on only a step above minimum wage had been an eye opening experience, even with the ridiculously cheap rent I owed Rhett.

"Usually you don't act like one. Rushing to get back to your crap job is acting like a kid."

"It's the only job I have, and I need it." Beggars can't be choosers in New York when it comes to making money with only a high school diploma and almost no previous work experience. Funny how working at a summer camp doesn't do much for a resume.

"Or you could pick a less expensive school and not worry so much about financial aid."

"Says the guy working on his PhD at NYU?"

"Hey, they pay me now." He opened the exterior door to our building.

"They didn't when you were an undergrad."

He let go of me so he could unlock the inner door. You had to tug on the door at the same time you turned the key or it didn't work. The super was supposed to fix the temperamental lock months before. "True, but my scholarship covered most of it."

I stood just inside the entryway. "All right, can't argue with that."

"Can you make it?" He gestured to the stairs. We lived in a third floor walkup.

"Maybe." I headed toward the stairs that currently looked like mountains. "It's worth a try."

Ten minutes later, I was propped up on the couch with a bottle of water. Rhett worried over me for another few minutes before I made him get back to work. I flipped through the channels, hoping for some random movie. There was absolutely nothing on, so I settled for the local news.

Another animal attack has been reported in Bryant Park. Authorities have not released the names of the victims, but once again citizens are urged to use caution when frequenting outdoor areas after dark.

I'd seen two other news reports just like it that week, although both reported attacks in different parts of the city. I thought of the wolf in the alley. It must have just been my overactive imagination messing with me. I needed sleep, and lots of it. I switched off the TV and closed my eyes. I didn't even have the energy to move to my room.

Soar **is available now!**

Made in the USA
Middletown, DE
21 July 2019